THE ADVENTURES OF TAMMY TROOT

LAVINIA DERWENT

Illustrated by
VIRGINIA SALTER

SPARROW
BOOKS

A Sparrow Book
Published by Arrow Books Limited
17–21 Conway Street, London W1P 6JD

An imprint of the Hutchinson Publishing Group

London Melbourne Sydney Auckland
Johannesburg and agencies
throughout the world

First published 1982

© Lavinia Derwent 1982

Set in Linoterm Plantin
by Book Economy Services
Burgess Hill, Sussex

Made and printed in Great Britain
by the Anchor Press Ltd
Tiptree, Essex

ISBN 0 09 927580 5

CONTENTS

1
MEET TAMMY TROOT

One morning a little fish woke up in a Scottish burn feeling very frisky and full of fun. He stood on the tip of his tail and cried, 'Tammy Troot speaking! That's me awake. The day can begin. I'm sure something exciting is going to happen.'

And he was right!

Something exciting was always happening to Tammy Troot. His Granny tried her best to keep

him under control. 'I wish you'd settle down, Tammy Troot, and lead a dull life like an ordinary fish,' she scolded.

But Tammy said, 'Hoots-toots! There's nothing ordinary about me, Granny. My head's bursting with brains. It's just a pity I'm so modest.'

'Modest!' grunted Rab Rat who was passing by. He flung his long tail over his shoulder in disgust. 'You're the biggest boaster in the burn. What do you say, Froggy?' he asked a frog who was huffing and puffing nearby.

'Nothing – puff – much.'

Froggy never said much. He was always half-asleep or half-awake, or puffing himself in and out.

But both he and Rab Rat were loyal friends, and so was Katy Kipper who did her best to attract Tammy's attention, though he did his best to dodge her. Then there were all the small fry who lived in the burn. Hundreds and thousands of tadpoles and tiddlers. All of them would have led dull lives if it had not been for the lively little fish and his brainwaves.

'I've got an idea,' said Tammy suddenly.

'Goodbye!' Rab Rat turned his tail on him, scenting danger.

'I pass,' wheezed Froggy and fell asleep standing on one leg.

But nothing would put Tammy off. 'Let's have a treasure-hunt in the Rubbish-Heap,' he suggested. 'You never know what we might find there. Maybe some valuable antiques.'

'My old scrubbing-brush,' cried Granny Troot. 'It's been missing for months. You can tidy up the Rubbish Heap while you're at it, Tammy Troot. It's the messiest mess I've ever seen.'

The Rubbish Heap was in an even messier mess by the time Tammy and his helpers had turned everything upside down. Pots, pans, pails, old boots, cocoa tins, empty bottles, bicycle wheels, cracked cups and teapots.

'Hooray! I've found a helicopter,' cried Tammy, rummaging amongst the rubbish.

'Stop telling tarradiddles, Tammy Troot,' grumped Rab Rat. 'It's just an old kettle.'

'Wait till you see what I'm going to do with it,' Tammy told him. 'A few screws here, a bit of wire there, and I'll soon be flying through the air with smoke coming out of the spout. No problem when you've got brains!'

'Wheesht!' interrupted Rab. 'I can hear a funny noise under all that junk.'

Tammy listened. 'It sounds like Froggy snoring. Mercy me! We must have burried the poor soul by mistake.'

The heap of junk began to heave, scattering pots and pans in all directions. 'Not to – puff – worry,' gasped Froggy. 'I've found a nice frying – puff – pan to snooze in. And look! Here's Granny's scrubbing – puff – brush.'

'Good for you, Froggy,' cried Tammy, patting him on the back. 'You've earned forty winks.'

'Fifty!' puffed Froggy, and fell fast asleep in the frying pan.

But the strange noise had not stopped. It was a weird wailing sound, as if someone was in distress.

'Come on, you lot,' called Tammy urgently. 'To the rescue!'

As they scrabbled feverishly amongst the junk the wailing grew louder and weirder. And suddenly they discovered a strange-looking object lying squashed at the bottom of the pile, screaming in agony.

Rab twirled his whiskers and backed out of its way. 'What on earth is that?' he puzzled. 'D'you think it's a bomb?'

'Don't be daft!' scoffed Tammy. 'It's a set of bagpipes.' He dug Froggy in the ribs. 'Wakey-wakey! Come on, Froggy. Use some of your puff to blow them up and we can all have a fling.'

Froggy sleepily huffed and puffed till the bag-pipes began to swell out and the wails gave way to

a stirring tune. 'Scotland the Brave'! The tadpoles and tiddlers marched up and down swinging their kilts, Katy Kipper danced the Highland Fling, and even Granny forgot her rheumatics, twirling round and round, crying, 'Hooch!'

Tammy Troot was on the tip of his tail dancing a reel when Froggy's breath gave out. The bagpipes let out a sigh and folded up. Then Tammy heard a distressed voice sobbing, 'Oh me! Oh deary me! What'll Nessie say if I don't get home to play her to sleep? Oh me! Oh deary deary me!'

Tammy stared at the bagpipes. 'Nessie! D'you mean the Loch Ness Monster?'

'Yes,' wailed the bagpipes. 'Oh me! Oh deary me! I've never missed a night. Don't know how I got here. Fell into a lorry full of junk, then I got pitched into the burn. How will I ever get back to Loch Ness? Oh deary deary deary . . . .'

'Stop moaning, Mr Bagpipes,' cried Tammy. 'I've got a brainwave. I'll give you a hitch home in my helicopter. Come on, everybody! All fins and paws to work. A wee screw here, and a wee bolt there, and we'll soon get the kettle flying.'

It was not as easy as all that, but when Tammy Troot's best brains got to work nothing was impossible. Before long the kettle began to shudder and shake, sparks started to fly, smoke came belching out of its spout and Tammy cried,

'That's it! We've got lift-off. Hang on, Mr Bag-pipes, and I'll get you home in two toots. T for Tammy's off on his trial run.'

The tadpoles and tiddlers raised a cheer as the kettle rose into the air with Mr Bagpipes clinging on to the handle. When he swelled out to his full size the merry strains of 'Scotland the Brave' were heard as Tammy flew high above the treetops and set course for Loch Ness.

It was an eventful journey with many ups and downs. Sometimes the kettle flew backwards, sometimes upside down, and sometimes it went into a spin and turned cartwheels in the air. They were chased by a flying saucer, they narrowly missed going slap-bang into a haystack and bumping into Ben Lomond. But at last the bag-pipes let out a screech of joy.

'Hip-hooch-hooray! I'm home! Look down, Tammy Troot. There's Nessie! See her humps in the loch. Hip-hooch-hooray! Are you going to drop in and say hullo?'

Tammy took a look at the Monster and gave a shiver. 'No! It would be safer to say goodbye. I'll just drop you here, Mr Bagpipes. Then T for Tammy's making straight home to the Rubbish Heap.'

Straight was not the right word. For suddenly the kettle boiled over and went whirling round

like a spinning-top. All the birds of the air came flying after it, calling 'Caw-caw! Whoo-whoo! Cuckoo! Here's a new bird. Let's peck it to pieces. Caw-caw! Whoo-whoo! Cuckoo!'

The little fish tugged dizzily at the controls and gasped, 'Jings! I'm in a tight corner! Anybody else would say this is the end, but Tammy Troot never gives in. Brainwave coming up!'

Hastily he pressed a lever which sent a blast of boiling water scooshing through the kettle spout. That did it! All the birds of the air flew off shaking their wet feathers and heading for the nearest wood where they all had nervous breakdowns.

Tammy was now in complete control of his helicopter, whizzing away home to the burn. And soon he saw a welcome sight. Granny's washing line hanging in the Rubbish Heap.

'Hooray!' he cheered, hovering overhead. 'Calling G for Granny. Mission completed! Another success for Tammy Troot. K for Kettle about to make a happy landing.'

2
TAMMY TROOT'S
SCHOOLDAYS

Tammy Troot was in his usual place at school. Where else but at the top of the class?

Froggy was at the bottom, sound asleep beside the tadpoles, tiddlers, and Backward Infants. The rest of the pupils at *Sam Sole's Academy for Mixed Fishes* were paying little attention to the teacher. A couple of eels were all-in wrestling under their desks. Rab Rat was making a catapult. And Katy Kipper, sitting behind Tammy, was whispering to him. 'Help me with my thumth. I'm thtuck.'

Tammy turned round and said, 'Oh you! You're always stuck. Can you not use your brains, like me?' At which point Mr Sole looked round from the blackboard and fixed an angry gaze on the little fish.

'Thomas Trout! Stop talking! Go to the bottom of the class. At once!'

Covered with shame Tammy pushed his way past Rab Rat who grunted, 'Oh, tough luck, Tammy Troot. Never mind! I'll be down to join you in a jiffy.'

As soon as the teacher's back was turned he put a piece of inky blotting-paper in his catapult and let fly. Ping! Straight to the target – the back of Mr Sam Sole's neck.

Mr Sole spun round. 'Who did that?' he roared, red in the face with anger. 'How dare you! Everybody go to the bottom of the class. At once!'

There was a great deal of shuffling and re-shuffling, at the end of which Tammy found himself back in his usual place at the top. But not for long.

Sam Sole was rapping his cane on the desk to attract attention. 'Sit up and listen. At once! We are having a very important visitor today. Professor Horace Halibut is coming to inspect the

school. So I want you all to be on your very best behaviour. Absolute silence!'

No sooner had he spoken than the absolute silence was broken by a voice which seemed to come from the direction of Tammy Troot.

'Silly old sausage! How d'you do! Silly old sausage!'

Everyone looked stunned. Mr Sole's face went purple with rage. 'HOW DARE YOU!' he roared in a furious voice. 'Who said that? Thomas Trout!'

'Oh no, sir! Not me, sir!' protested Tammy. 'I'd never dream of calling you a silly old anything. Not guilty!' But Mr Sole would not listen to him.

'The bottom of the class!' he raged. 'If I hear another word I'll punish the lot of you. Absolute silence!'

Once more Tammy had to make the journey down to join the Backward Infants. And once more the absolute silence was broken.

'Silly old sausage! How d'you do! Silly old sausage!'

It was too much for the teacher. Grasping his cane, he began to whack his desk to show that he meant business. 'Thomas Trout!' he roared in a terrifying voice. 'Come out and get punished! I'm going to make you suffer.'

There was a gasp from the pupils. Katy Kipper fell down in a faint. Then at that moment Tammy caught sight of something moving, and hastily put up his fin. 'Please, sir, it's a budgie, sir,' he told the teacher. 'Look, Mr Sole, sir. There he is, behind the blackboard.'

And there he was – a small excited budgie – fluttering about and repeating all the phrases he had learnt off by heart. 'Pretty boy! Humpty Dumpty had a great fall! Silly old sausage! How d'you do! Silly old sausage!'

Mr Sole was growing frantic. 'Get that bird out before the Professor comes,' he ordered. 'Thomas Trout, open the door. Shoo! Get out! We must have absolute silence. OUT!'

But the budgie was enjoying himself and had no intention of being ordered out. He flew round and round the classroom with all the pupils giving chase. The place was in such an uproar that no one noticed a stranger who had come in. Professor Horace Halibut. Very stout, very angry, and very shocked at such a sight.

'DIS-GRACE-FUL!' he cried out. 'Mr Sole I'm surprised at you! Surprised and ashamed! Is this the way you run your school? It's DIS-GRACE-FUL! Where is your discipline?'

A chirpy voice answered him. 'Silly old sausage! How d'you do! Silly old sausage!'

17

Professor Horace Halibut looked as if he was about to explode. 'DIS-GRACE-FUL!' he burst out. 'Mr Sole, I shall have you expelled for your impudence. You are not fit to run a school for Mixed Fishes . . . .'

'Silly old sausage!' interrupted the voice.

By now Mr Sole had completely lost control and gone to hide behind the blackboard. So Tammy Troot decided it was time he came forward to explain.

'Please, Mr Professor, sir, it's a budgie, sir. Usually we're perfect pupils and Mr Sole's a first-

class teacher. He always insists on absolute silence. . . .'

Just then a loud buzzing was heard as another intruder flew into the classroom. A large, fat bumble-bee.

'BUZZZZ! Make way for the Queen Bee and her followers. They're coming in their hundreds and thousands, looking for a place to swarm. This will do fine. We'll settle here. BUZZZZZ!'

The sight of a hundred thousand bees flying in at the door was enough to send everyone scuttling to join Mr Sole behind the blackboard. Including

the Professor, who looked the most terrified of the lot. Everyone, that is, except Tammy Troot, who was always at his best in an emergency. Something must be done and *he* would do it.

'Leave this to me and my brains. I'll be back in two toots,' he cried and dodged past the Queen Bee who was flying in with a crown on her head. Then he dashed away down the burn, breaking the speed record.

As luck would have it, the first person he met was Granny Troot on her way to open a bazaar in aid of Hard-up and Homeless Fishes. She was wearing her best flowery hat and practising her speech.

Bowing to an imaginary audience she mumbled, 'Fellow Fishes, I have the most greatest pleasure in telling you about this most goodest cause.' She was about to go on when suddenly, to her surprise, her hat was whipped off her head.

'Tammy Troot!' she cried out in a shocked voice. 'What d'you think you're up to? My best hat! Give it back. . . .'

But Tammy was already making off with it. 'Sorry, Granny, but I need your hat in an even gooder cause. You'll just have to make a bare-headed speech, and the best of luck. Explanations later.'

And he raced back to the classroom with his trophy.

At the sight of Granny's flowery hat the Queen Bee came flying towards him, fluttering her wings with pleasure. 'Oh! I like that!' she buzzed. She looked almost dizzy with joy. 'It's rather sweet! Just my style! Let's settle here. BUZZZZZ!.'

As she landed on the hat Tammy bowed to her and said, 'It's all yours, Your Majesty. But maybe you'd be healthier in the open air. So d'you mind if I take you and the hat away to a quiet corner of the Rubbish Heap? Come on, the rest of you. Follow me and Her Majesty.'

Away he went, followed by swarms of buzzing bees, and deposited Granny's hat safely in a secluded corner of the Rubbish Heap. 'Who knows? Perhaps it'll be improved by the time Granny gets it back. It never suited her, anyway,' thought the little fish as he hurried back to the schoolroom.

He was pleased to hear the budgie chirping from a nearby tree. 'How d'you do! Clever old sausage! Well done, Tammy Troot – toot – toot.'

He was even more pleased when he went inside and heard the whole class cheering him.

Professor Horace Halibut came out from behind the blackboard to shake him by the fin. 'Good for you! Top of the class! Mr Sole, I congratulate you on having such a bright pupil. For his sake, I'll give the school full marks. And a half-holiday.'

As the cheers grew louder Tammy looked modestly down at his tail. 'Och, it's nothing,' he told the Professor. 'What's the good of having brains if I don't use them? I've got plenty more where they came from.'

3
TAMMY TROOT, PRIVATE EYE

One dark night a furtive figure could be seen slinking towards the Rubbish Heap. Who could it be?

Tammy Troot, Private Eye!

There had been a spate of burglaries in the burn. Even Granny's bottle of rheumatic-mixture had been stolen, and PC Cod was at his wits' end. Which was not very far!

So Tammy Troot had decided to solve the crimes himself with the aid of his brains and a pair of small scissors borrowed from Granny's work-basket. It was the only weapon he could find.

'Whoo – hoo – hoo!'

The little fish almost jumped out of his skin as an owl gave an eerie hoot. 'Be b-brave!' Tammy told himself. 'Think of Sh-Sherlock Thing-ummy.'

Just then he saw a light darting here and there in the sky, but it was only Willy Wisp up to his tricks, trying to lead everyone astray. 'You can't fool me, Willy Wisp,' said Tammy, taking no notice of him. The next moment he bumped into someone who grabbed him in a grip of iron.

'Got you!' a gruff voice cried. 'I arrest you in the name of the law.'

'Don't be daft, PC Cod,' said Tammy, wriggling free. 'It's just me. Tammy Troot, Private Eye.'

The policeman let Tammy go. Then he pushed his helmet to the back of his head and said, 'Och well! If you're on night-duty, laddie, I might as well go home to my bed.' And away he plodded, leaving Tammy to patrol the burn on his own.

Tammy was bending down searching for clues under a stone when he heard someone breathing heavily behind him. His heart went thump-thud-thump! Could this be the criminal? 'Courage, Tammy Troot!' he told himself. 'Action!'

He whipped round and found himself facing a tom cat with a sack over his shoulder. A Cat Burglar!

'Stand and deliver!' said Tammy boldly and pointed the scissors at the thief. 'The game's up!'

'Grrr!' The Cat Burglar growled at him and put out a paw to pick him up. 'Your game's up! I'll pop you into my swag bag. You'll make a tasty titbit once I've stolen some more loot. Grrr! In you go!'

And in went Tammy head first, landing beside the stolen goods in the sack. Granny's bottle of rheumatic-mixture, Rab Rat's mouth-organ, Froggy's water-pistol and Katy Kipper's handbag. 'Jings! I'll have to get out of here at the toot,' thought the little fish. 'Thank goodness, I've still got my brains. And Granny's scissors.'

Quick as lightning he snipped a hole in the bottom of the sack and slipped safely through, back into the burn. The Cat Burglar was prowling away downstream with the sack on his back, little knowing that his titbit had escaped.

What next? Tammy puzzled his brains and did some quick thinking. Willy Wisp was still flitting about the night sky. Suddenly Tammy had an idea.

'Wi – lly! Willy Wisp!' he called urgently. 'Do me a favour. See that Cat Burglar? Light his way

towards the Rubbish Heap, like a good chap. There's an empty bird-cage there. Try to lure him into it, and I'll be back in two toots to lock him up.'

'Okay!' called Willy Wisp and darted away after the burglar.

Meantime Tammy was darting off in the opposite direction, towards Granny's clothes-line. One of her white nightgowns was hanging there. 'Just the job!' thought Tammy. He reached up to pull it down and then hurried towards the Rubbish Heap.

He could hear Willy Wisp calling to the Cat Burglar, who was stumbling about in the dark-ness. 'This way! Follow me . . . .' Then he heard the thief blundering into the bird-cage. Willy Wisp had done his job well!

Tammy put on a spurt and slammed the door of the cage shut. Then he wriggled himself into Granny's nightgown.

'Grrr!' The Cat Burglar was beating frantically at the bars of the cage. 'What's up? Where am I? Let me out! Open the door!'

Willy Wisp flew off chuckling to himself. The owl called 'Whoo-hoo-hoo!' and a ghostly figure reared up in front of the cage, waving its white arms and saying in an unearthly voice, 'Beware! I have come to haunt you. Beware!'

The Cat Burglar let out a cry of terror and crouched at the back of the cage, shivering and shaking with fright. His fur stood on end and his teeth began to chatter till he could scarcely speak. There was not even a 'Grrr' left in him.

'A g-g-ghost!' he gasped, trembling so much that the cage rattled and shook. 'Go away! Don't come near me! Help! Save me! I'm t-t-t-terrified!'

But the white figure came nearer and nearer, 'Beware!' it repeated. 'This is the ghost of Tammy Troot, come to warn you to mend your ways. You will be haunted for the rest of your life. Unless you are sorry for your sins. Beware!'

By now the burglar was almost fainting with fear. 'S-S-Sorry!' he shivered. 'Yes, yes, I'm sorry! I'll never do anything wrong again, Never! I'll give back everything I've stolen and go straight for the rest of my life. I p-p-promise. Only stop haunting me, p-p-please. I'm t-t-t-terrified!'

The ghost gave him another warning. 'Beware! I could fetch a policeman and he'd give you a life-sentence. Or would you rather be haunted for ever and ever?'

'No, No! Have pity, p-p-please!' pleaded the prisoner. 'Let me go. I've learned my l-l-lesson.'

He looked so pathetic that the ghost's heart began to soften. 'Right! I believe you have learned your lesson,' he said, opening the cage door. 'Out! But if you ever come back to the burn you'll have to reckon with Tammy Troot's ghost. Wi – lly! Willy Wisp! Show a light!'

'Okay!' chuckled Willy Wisp, flitting about in the sky. 'Leave him to me, Tammy Troot. I'll lead him a dance! Come this way, Mr ex-Burglar. This way. . . .'

The Cat took to his heels, dropping the sack of stolen goods and following the flickering light in the sky. Willy Wisp led him here, there and everywhere. Tammy Troot never knew where he landed, but at least he kept his promise and was never seen again in the burn.

'Thanks to me and my brains,' thought the little fish, picking up the swag bag. 'Granny'll be awful glad to get back her rheumatic-mixture.'

He had almost reached home when someone suddenly pounced on him and grabbed the bag out of his grasp.

'I arrest you in the name of the law!' said a gruff voice.

'Not again, PC Cod!' cried Tammy, wriggling out of his clutch. 'I thought you were off duty having your beauty sleep.'

'I couldn't sleep for thinking of the burglar,' grumbled the policeman, pushing back his helmet. 'What's in that bag, laddie?'

Virginia Salter.

'Stolen goods,' Tammy told him. 'You can have the job of delivering them back to their owners. Tammy Troot, Private Eye, has done his job. And if Scotland Yard's ever looking for an expert you can let them know where to find me.'

4
TAMMY TROOT'S KETTLE

One day a strange sound was heard in the burn. Tammy Troot was taking off in his helicopter which he had invented himself from an old kettle he had found in the Rubbish Heap.

'It's great to have brains,' thought the little fish as the kettle shot into the air with sparks flying

and smoke puffing from its spout. 'This beats a flying saucer. T for Tammy calling G for Granny. This is me away on a mystery tour in the sky. Are you receiving me?'

'Loud and clear.' A babble of voices answered him. 'R for Rab Rat.' 'F for– puff – Froggy.' 'K for Katy Kipper.' Mixed up with tadpoles and tiddlers who all wanted their voices to be heard. But the loudest and clearest of the lot was G for Granny.

'You behave yourself, Tammy Troot,' she scolded. 'Remember the sky-way code, and be sure to bring that kettle home in time for tea.'

'Righto, Granny. Message received. Over and out.'

Tammy was soaring above the treetops when he heard a warning shout from the Pigeon Postman. 'Steady on, Tammy Troot,' he grumped. 'You've taken off one of my tail feathers.'

'Sorry, Postie.' Tammy slowed down and stared at the pigeon's bulging postbag. 'Mercy me! what a heavy load.'

The postman's wings drooped wearily. 'It's you and your fan-mail, Tammy Troot,' he complained. 'It gets bigger every day.'

'I can't help being so popular,' sighed the little fish. 'And so modest! Never mind, Postie. I'll take the letters from you to lighten your load.'

The pigeon thankfully dropped the bundle of mail into the helicopter. And now he was left with an odd-looking parcel tied up in brown paper and string.

'Who is that for?' Tammy asked.

'Goodness knows!' The Postie put on his spectacles and peered at the parcel. 'The label's fallen off. Perfect pest! I'll have to carry it all the way back to the post-office.'

'No, you won't.' Tammy had a better idea. 'Leave it to me and my brains. I'll find a home for it, Postie.' And he took the parcel into the helicopter. 'It'll be my good deed for the day.'

'Ta, Tammy Troot.' The Postie sighed with relief. 'I'll write a fan-letter to you myself some day.' He hitched up his postbag, which was much lighter by now. 'That's good! I've only got one thing left to deliver. A birthday card for old Mrs Owl. No bother. Ta-ta, Tammy Troot, and happy landings.'

But Tammy had no intention of landing yet. He twirled the controls inside the kettle to get up speed, and went zooming high into the clouds. 'Toot-toot! Calling the Concorde. Keep out of the way. Tammy Troot's flying sky-high.'

He was in the middle of a fluffy white cloud when he heard a strange sound coming from the parcel. 'Tick-tick-tick!'

Tammy's tail began to tremble with fright. 'Oh jings! It sounds like a time-bomb. I'd better throw it overboard before it explodes. That would be the end of this kettle, not to mention me.'

By now the parcel had begun to make a whirring noise. Then Tammy heard a voice calling, 'Cuckoo! Cuckoo! Cuckoo!'

'Bless my brains! It's a cuckoo clock.' What a relief! Now all he had to do was deliver it to someone. The problem was who and where?

He hovered and hesitated for a moment while he was puzzling it out. Then he heard, 'Oo-cuck! Oo-cuck! Oo-cuck! You're going backwards. Charlie Cuckoo here. Straight on, please. Oo-cuck!'

'Sorry, Charlie.' Tammy straightened up and went whirling away in the kettle keeping a steady course. But suddenly he looked back and saw that he was being followed.

Hundreds of cuckoos were chasing after him. The air was thick with birds all calling 'Cuck-cuck-cuck-oo! Stop! Wait for us. We want a nest, too. Give us a lift. Cuck-cuck-cuck-oo!'

The parcel began to quiver and quake. Charlie Cuckoo seemed to be in a great state of terror.

'Hurry up! Hurry up-up-UP!' he urged Tammy 'They'll peck me to pieces if they catch me. They must think I've found a nice nest, and they're all jealous. Hurry up-up-UP! Quick-oo! Quick-oo! Quick-oo!'

'I'll be as quick as lightning,' promised Tammy. 'Fasten your seat-belt, Charlie. I'm going to loop the loop, then I'll put out a smoke-screen to shake them off. T for Tammy going into action.'

And with that Tammy sent the kettle spinning up, down and roundabout, getting up so much speed that the birds were almost blinded by the steam coming from the spout. Then he zig-zagged away and hid behind a dark cloud.

'Cuck-cuck-cuck-oo!' In the distance he could hear the disappointed cuckoos holding a committee-meeting. 'We've lost the flying nest. What can we do? We'd better turn back and look elsewhere. Back! Turn back! Cuck-cuck-cuck-oo!' Then he heard a flutter of wings as they all flew away.

'All clear!' called Tammy, patting himself on the back. 'How are you, Charlie? Alive and kicking?'

'Oo-cuck! Upside down and inside out, but safe and sound, thanks to you, Mr Troot.' Charlie Cuckoo tried to clap his wings inside the parcel. 'Three cheers for you. I think you're wonderful.'

'Yes, I know,' agreed Tammy. 'You're a good judge of character. Now then, Charlie, the next item on the programme is to find a nice home for you. Hold on till I puzzle my brains.'

It did not take the little fish long. Suddenly he

cried out, 'Got it! How would you like to be a birthday present?'

'Cuckoo! Who would want me?'

'Old Mrs Owl,' Tammy told him. 'She's a wee bit deaf and a wee bit blind, and she never knows what time it is. So you'd be the best birthday present she's ever had. And what's more, Charlie, she's got a nice cosy nest with plenty of room. You could share it with her and be happy ever after. What d'you think of that for a Tammy Troot special?'

There was no doubt that Charlie Cuckoo thought it a good idea. Indeed, he was so delighted that he nearly went mad with joy. He rustled the brown paper. He undid the knots with his beak. Then he poked out his head and called, 'CUCK-OO-OO! This is the luckiest day in my life. I'm the happiest cuckoo in the world. Fancy finding a home! All thanks to you, Mr Troot.' He clapped his wings with delight. 'CUCK-OO!'

'Dry up, Charlie,' Tammy warned him. 'You'd better keep quiet or we'll have all those cuckoos chasing after us again. Old Mrs Owl has only room for one lodger. Hold your breath and hang on to your feathers. Going down!'

And he came out from behind the cloud and set course for the treetops near the burn. Down, down! 'A wee bit to the right, Tammy,' he told

himself. 'Now a wee bit to the left. That's it! We're here!'

Old Mrs Owl was sitting snugly in her nest, trying to read her birthday card, when the helicopter came hovering overhead.

'Many happy returns, Mrs Owl,' called Tammy as he guided the kettle closer to her nest. 'I've brought an extra-special birthday present for you.'

'Oh my! That's very kind of you, Tammy Troot,' said old Mrs Owl, fluffing out her feathers. 'Have you any idea what the time is?'

'Teatime!' chirped Charlie Cuckoo, bursting out of the brown paper parcel. He flew into the nest and snuggled down beside her. 'Happy birthday to you, Mrs Owl. Cuckoo! Cuckoo! And happy landings to me. There's no place like home. Cuck-cuck-OOOOOOO!'

'Home! That reminds me. I'd better send a message to Granny.' Tammy Troot waved good-bye to Mrs Owl and her new lodger who were settling down happily together. 'T for Tammy coming home for his tea. The kettle's boiling. Over and out!'

5
TAMMY TROOT SWIMS THE CHANNEL

'Toot-toot! Watch out! This is me. Make way for Tammy Troot. Toot-toot!'

Tammy Troot came swimming at high speed up the burn.

The tadpoles and tiddlers scurried out of his way as he shot past. Mrs Sprat dropped her shopping bag, and PC Cod blew a warning blast on his whistle. But Tammy was well away, leaving only a ripple in the water.

He was making straight for the Rubbish Heap where Granny Troot was hanging out the washing. Rab Rat was putting his whiskers in curlers, and Froggy was snoozing in an old frying-pan. It was a peaceful scene till Tammy arrived.

'Danger!' Rab Rat flung his long tail over his shoulder. 'Take cover! Here comes Tammy Troot and his brains.'

Granny took a clothes-peg out of her mouth and cried, 'Watch it, Tammy Troot! You'll be fined for dangerous swimming. What d'you think you're doing?'

'The breast-stroke,' said Tammy, putting on his brakes. 'And the crawl.' He stood on his tail and announced, 'I'm getting ready to swim the Channel. Are you not proud of me, Granny?'

'No,' said Granny. 'I think you're daft.'

'Hear hear!' agreed Rab, putting in another curler.

'Hear – puff – hear!' breathed Froggy, half asleep.

'Stick-in-the-muds!' scoffed Tammy. 'Wait till you read about it on the front page of the *Troots' and Tiddlers' Gazette*. FAMOUS FISH BREAKS RECORD. Maybe you'll get your pictures in, too. And I'll be on television. I might even get knighted. "Arise, Sir Thomas Trout!"'

'You and your modesty!' grunted Rab. 'Dry

up, Tammy Troot. Away you go and forget to come back.'

But it did not take Tammy long to persuade them to accompany him to Dover to give him a send-off.

Granny took in the washing and put a bottle of rheumatic-mixture in her pocket. 'Goodness knows what Dr Haddock would say if he knew I was gallivanting away to a foreign land. Me and my pains!'

But Tammy said, 'Hoots-toots! England's not foreign. I'm the one who'll have to speak a different language. French. Once I've crossed the Channel. Come on, Froggy. Wakey-wakey!'

Froggy opened a sleepy eye and wheezed, 'Is it morning already? I haven't slept a – puff – wink all night. Is this a dream, Tammy – puff – Troot?'

'No, it's a nightmare,' said Rab Rat, taking out his curlers. 'Lead on, Tammy Troot. The sooner we see you off the better.'

They had at least a hundred adventures on the way. Maybe a thousand. And by the time they reached the English Channel Granny's bottle was half empty. There was not a curl left in Rab's whiskers and Froggy was walking in his sleep.

But Tammy Troot was as frisky as ever when he reared himself up to make his farewell speech.

'Cheerio, everybody, I don't know how you'll

get on without me, but you'll need to try your best.'

'Good – puff – bye,' wheezed Froggy.

'Good riddance!' grunted Rab Rat.

'Ta-ta, Tammy Troot,' said Granny with a sigh of relief. 'Don't hurry back.'

Tammy gave them a final wave and dived into the deep waters of the Channel. 'Mercy me! it's colder than the burn,' shivered the little fish. 'Och well! I'll just have to swim faster to keep warm.'

He changed gear and swam so fast that soon he was far away from the white cliffs of Dover. He met many strange creatures on the way. Sea-horses running races. Sword-fish fighting duels. Jellyfish shivering and shaking. And suddenly he heard someone speaking French.

'Cheers! I must be getting near the other side. Well done, me!'

Just then a glamorous French fish swam up to him, fluttering her eyelashes. 'Oo-la-la! How do you do? I am Fifi. You are Engleesh?'

'Scottish! Tammy Troot Esquire in a hurry. Hullo Fifi, and goodbye.'

Tammy dived under a wave to dodge her, but when he came up he found someone pushing him aside. A large American fish smoking a cigar.

'Out of the way! Gee! Can't you see I'm swimming the Channel for the United States?'

'Me too, for Scotland!' Tammy told him. 'I'll challenge you to a race, Mr USA.'

'Huh! I'll soon beat a little tiddler like you!'

They were swimming neck and neck when suddenly they heard a scream.

'It sounds like Fifi in trouble,' said Tammy, slowing up to listen.

'Gee! I ain't gonna bother with no dame in distress.' The American flicked his cigar ash at Tammy and hurried past him. 'You've lost the race, tiddler.'

Never mind the race. Tammy could not ignore the calls for help. 'SOS! Oo-la-la! HELP!'

'Hang on, Fifi!' The little fish turned and swam back. 'Tammy Troot to the rescue!'

Not a moment too soon. He was just in time to find Fifi, fainting with fright, in the clutches of a fearsome octopus. Tammy almost fainted, too, at the sight of such a monster. But he braced himself up and told himself to be brave. Then he swam up to the Octopus.

'Look here, Mr. Octopus, sir,' he said, trying not to shiver with fear. 'Let go at once or I'll – I'll p-punch your n-nose.'

The octopus gave a great roar of rage. 'WHAT? Come closer then!' He whipped out one of his arms and caught Tammy in a grip of iron.

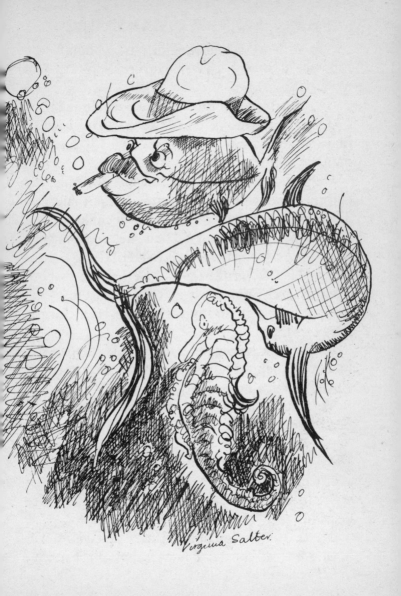

Virginia Salter.

'Oh d-dear!' Tammy squirmed about in the monster's grasp. 'The f-future looks awful unsettled.'

'Oo-la-la!' wailed Fifi. 'We're both done for!'

This was the moment for Tammy to have one of his brilliant brainwaves. 'I know! I'll find the octopus's funny-bone.'

He twisted around and began to tickle the octopus under one of his arms. Instant success! To Tammy's delight the monster began to giggle. 'Ho-ho-ho! He-he-he!' Then he roared with laughter. 'HO-HO-HO! HE-HE-HE! I'll split my sides!' He writhed about, letting go of both Tammy and Fifi. 'Must go to the bottom of the sea and have a good laugh. HO-HO-HO! Gurgle-gurgle-gurgle!'

As he sank below the surface Fifi clapped her fins with delight. 'Oo-la-la! You are the most clever fish in all the world,' she told Tammy.

'Agreed,' said Tammy modestly, 'but you'll need to cut the praises short, Fifi. I'm off at the toot.'

And off at the toot went Tammy, zig-zagging to avoid his admirer. Then he put on the biggest spurt in his life. 'Faster, Tammy, faster! You're nearly there!'

There was no sign of his American rival. 'He'll have gone off-course, I hope,' thought Tammy, racing the waves and overtaking a steamer. Then he let out a cry of triumph. 'Hooray! I can see France. Oh me! Oh my! Am I not the boy! Tammy Troot swims the Channel in record time.'

He was disappointed that there were no cheering crowds to welcome him. Only three figures huddled together on the shore.

'Mercy me! It's Granny and Rab and Froggy. However did you get to France?'

'France!' Granny drank the last drop from her bottle. 'We've never budged from the beach since you left, and now I've got cramp to keep my rheumatics company.'

The awful truth dawned on Tammy. In dodging Fifi he had turned completely round and swum back to his home port.

'Och well! It saves the return journey,' he consoled himself. 'And nobody can say I haven't swum the Channel, for I've been more than half-way there and back, and done a good deed in between. It proves that, win or lose, I'm a good sportsman. So three cheers for Tammy Troot! For I'm a jolly good fellow!'

6
TAMMY TROOT'S PARTY

Granny Troot was knitting a new shawl to keep her rheumatics warm and listening-in to Fishy Favourites on the Bee Bee Cee – the Burn Broadcasting Corporation – when an agitated voice broke in.

'I say! I say! Special announcement! Here is a gale warning. Take cover, everybody. I say! I say! I'm going to be blown off the air. SOS! Drop everything! I say! I say. . . .!'

Granny took him at his word and dropped a stitch. But Tammy Troot rose to the occasion and took command as usual.

'Action stations!' he called out, standing on the tip of his tail. 'Make your way to the cave. It's the safest place to shelter. Come along, Granny. Bring your knitting and your rheumatics. Hurry! No time to waste. The wind's rising already. Toot-toot! Follow Tammy Troot.'

He began to round up the tadpoles and tiddlers. Not a moment too soon. The gale had gathered force, and all the junk in the Rubbish Heap was flying through the air. Including Froggy, asleep in an old teapot, and Rab Rat

practising 'Pop Goes the Weasel' on his mouth-
organ.

It was difficult to avoid a direct hit. Tammy
tried to dodge cocoa tins, pan lids, flying cups and
saucers, as well as Susie Sole who had been tossed
into the air and was doing the splits above his
head. But at last he got everyone safely into the
shelter of the cave.

Mrs Swan was there with her feathers ruffled
inside out; Katy Kipper, whose perm was almost
blown off her head, and the Bee Bee Cee announcer, who wailed, 'I say! I say! I'll never be
the same again.'

'Good!' said Tammy, pushing him aside.

'That's one blessing! Are we all present and correct?'

It was so dark inside the cave that no one was sure if they were present or correct. But Tammy Troot soon put that right.

'Glow-worms! Forward, please! Switch on your lights.'

When the cave was lit up Tammy barred the door to keep out the gale. Then he cried, 'Come on, everybody. Forget the storm. We might as well enjoy ourselves and have a party. Or a Celebrity Concert. Anyone here with talent, apart from me?'

He had plenty of offers. So many that it was difficult to know where to start. Everyone wanted to perform, from the smallest minnow to the oldest eel. Katy Kipper fancied herself as a ballerina. Susie Sole started to rock and roll. Rab Rat played 'Pop Goes the Weasel' on his mouth-organ and then recited 'A Rat's A Rat for a' That'. Froggy gave a perfect imitation of a frog sleepwalking. Granny showed everyone her rheumatics. And even the Bee Bee Cee announcer wanted to get into the act.

'I say! I say! I'm very good at being Big Ben. DING-DONG! DING-DONG. . . .!'

Tammy Troot acted as Master of Ceremonies and tried his best to keep everyone in order. It was not easy, especially when thousands of tadpoles and tiddlers all wanted to sing at the same time.

'QUIET!' he shouted out. 'Hold on! Brainwave coming up. I tell you what. Let's have community singing, then you'll all get a chance to join in, whether you've got a voice or not. Mind! I've got some great ideas, though I say it myself.'

The little fish borrowed one of Granny's knitting-needles to use as a baton and began to conduct the company in a medley of rousing songs. Medley was the right word. The din nearly raised the roof, for the small fry all wanted their own favourite tunes. So some were singing 'Jingle Bells' while others were shouting out 'Three Blind Mice', or trilling 'Over the Sea to Skye'. But at least they made plenty of sound and drowned out the noise of the gale raging outside.

Rab Rat did his best to accompany them on his mouth-organ, and Froggy puffed himself in and out in time with the conductor's baton. Even Granny sang 'Tra-la-la' now and again, and the announcer cried, 'I say! I say! I'll have to record you for the Bee Bee Cee.'

They were singing merrily in the midst of 'Rule Britannia' mixed up with 'Scotland the Brave' when there was a sudden loud noise at the cave door.

Thump! Thump! Thump!

The music suddenly tailed off, ending in a squeal from Katy Kipper. But Tammy's baton did not waver. 'Sing on!' he cried, still beating time. 'I'll go and see who it is. Britons never-never-never shall be slaves!'

He needed all his courage when he opened the door and saw who was facing him. A large hungry Crocodile snapping his sharp teeth. 'Snip-snap! Snip-snap!'

'Full up!' said Tammy hastily. 'No more room. Goodbye, Mr Croc-oc-ocodile.' And he tried to shut the door on the intruder. But the Crocodile pushed him aside, and in he came.

'Snip-snap!' he cried, looking around him, and licking his lips. 'That's good! I can see I'm going to enjoy my supper tonight. Snip-snap! I'll start with you,' he said, rounding on Tammy Troot. 'You'll make a tasty first course.'

Everybody gasped with terror, but Tammy remained calm. He had been in many tight corners before, and he knew he had to do some quick thinking if he was to save himself and all the others. So his brain began to work overtime.

'Right-o, Mr C-Crocodile. I'm ready,' he said, pretending not to be worried. 'Good appetite! I hope you'll enjoy your supper. But first I'd like to show you what I can do with my magic wand. Watch this!'

He waved Granny's knitting-needle in the air and called in a loud voice, 'Lights out!' The glow-worms obediently switched off their lights, leaving the cave in pitch darkness. Tammy could hear the Crocodile giving a gasp and snip-snapping his teeth in surprise.

'Not to worry, Mr Crocodile. I'll soon mend the fuse,' Tammy told him. 'I'll just wave my wand and shout, "Lights on"!' Once more the glow-worms obeyed his command and the cave was lit up.

The Crocodile was blinking his eyes and looking amazed at Tammy's magic tricks.

'Oh, that's nothing, Mr Crocodile,' said Tammy cunningly. 'I'll give you another demonstration. It'll whet your appetite for your supper. Would you like me to make *you* disappear? It'll be no trouble. But I'm not sure if I could bring you back again. Or I could try turning you into a turnip. Or a sausage, maybe. Just say the word and I'll oblige.'

He was about to wave the knitting-needle again when the Crocodile hastily backed towards the door. 'No! No thanks!' His teeth were now snip-snapping with fright. 'S-Stop waving that w-wand. This is no p-place for me. I'll do without my s-s-supper. G-G-Goodbye!'

'Cheerio, Mr Crocodile,' Tammy called after

him. 'Thanks for dropping in. And dropping out!'

Everyone in the cave began to cheer him. 'Hip-hip-HOORAY! A hundred cheers for Tammy Troot and his brains.' The glow-worms twinkled their lights on and off to show how pleased they were. Then all the company began to dance round Tammy, who bowed modestly to them and said, 'Och! I know I deserve it, but save your breath for the Eightsome Reel. Take back your knitting-needle, Granny. It's come in very handy. And come and be my partner. It'll do your rheumatics a world of good. Blow your mouth-organ, Rab Rat, and away we go!'

They were dancing merrily round the cave when the announcer cried, 'I say! I say! The gale's died down. I'd better get back to the Bee Bee Cee.'

'You do that,' Tammy told him. 'We'll try not to miss you.'

And they didn't. On they danced till everyone was as breathless as Froggy, and Tammy called, 'Last waltz! All good things come to an end. Except me! I go on for ever.'

7
TAMMY TROOT'S WHIRLPOOL

It all began with the telephone ringing in the Rubbish Heap. *Ting-a-ling-a-ling.*

'Tammy Troot!' cried Granny, who was bathing her rheumatics in an old tin tub and could not be seen for soap suds. 'What are you doing?'

'Nothing,' said Tammy.

'Well, stop it at once and answer the telephone.'

'Right-o, Granny.' Tammy hurried to obey. He lifted the receiver and said in his Sunday voice, 'Rubbish Heap 1212. The Right Honourable Thomas Trout speaking. Over!'

There was a pause. 'Who is it?' called Granny Troot from the bath-tub.

'It's a long distance,' Tammy told her.

'Where to?' asked Granny.

'Don't know,' said the little fish. 'It's just a faraway voice saying a VIP's coming to visit us.'

'What's a VIP?'

'A Very Important Person. Like me,' explained Tammy. 'It might be royalty.'

'Mercy me!' Granny was out of the tub in a flash, rheumatics and all. 'Here, Tammy Troot,

you'd better jump in and have a scrub. If it's royalty they might inspect you from top to tail. In you go!'

She pushed Tammy into the tub and hurried away to look out her best shawl and her feather boa. Then she came back to ask him, 'D'you think I should wear a hat or put on a tiara?'

There was no reply. 'Tammy Troot, are you deaf?' cried Granny and went to peer into the bathtub. It was empty except for some frothy water. Where was Tammy Troot?

Flying through the air, clinging desperately to a large soap bubble which had been blown sky-high, that's where.

'Never a dull moment!' gasped the little fish.

'Oh dear! What's going to happen when the b-bubble b-bursts? I can't see where I'm going, I've got so much s-soap in my eyes.'

Just then the bubble burst with a 'plop' and down tumbled Tammy, head over tail. Going! Going! SPLASH!

'Oh! lucky me!' cried Tammy. 'I've landed in water!'

Not so lucky! When he rubbed his eyes and looked around him, he found he was not back in the burn but in a horse-trough in a farmyard. A large thirsty horse was leaning over the trough to lap up the water.

'Wheee!' cried the horse, blowing down his nose. 'There's something fishy about this water today. And something soapy, too. Wheee! But I'm so thirsty I'm going to drink every drop. Wheee!'

'Help! not *every* drop, I hope,' thought Tammy, swimming hastily into a corner to keep out of the way. Soon he began to gasp for breath as the horse gulped down great mouthfuls of water. There was scarcely a trickle left before he stopped.

'Oh jings! I f-feel like a f-fish out of water,' thought Tammy, floundering about in distress. 'But I'm not giving in. I'll cross my fins and hope for a miracle.'

Suddenly to his relief the miracle happened. Something came plopping down from the sky. 'A raindrop!' cheered Tammy. It was quickly followed by another and another. And then the shower became a deluge, filling up the trough and drenching the horse.

'Wheee!' he cried, kicking up his heels and shaking off the rain. 'I'm getting soaked to the skin. And me out without my brolly! Wheee! I'm away into the stable before I catch the sneezes. Wheee! ATISHOOO!'

And away he clumped, leaving Tammy floating about in the trough. There was too much water in it now, so much that it began to overflow and swept Tammy overboard.

Luckily the rain was still pouring down and he was able to swim away in a trickling stream through the farmyard. But it was a dangerous journey, for the cocks and hens came splashing after him, and a large turkey cried, 'Gobble-gob-ble-gobble! Here's a nice tasty bite for my empty tum. Hold on! I'm going to gobble-gobble you up. Wait!'

'Can't wait, Mr Gobbler. I'm in a hurry!' cried Tammy and swirled safely past him.

In any case, he had to go where the downpour swept him. And soon he was swimming out of the farmyard, delighted to find he was aiming straight for a small stream. His own burn!

'Toot-toot!' cried the frisky little fish. 'All's well with the world. Tammy Troot's on his way home.'

But he had to change his tune when he found himself being tossed headfirst into a whirlpool. It was like being in a spin-dryer. Round and round, faster and faster whirled Tammy. 'I'll bump into myself, if I don't look out,' he gasped. 'I'm coming and going at the same time.'

All of a sudden he was aware of someone whirling round in the opposite direction. Every time they passed each other the stranger let out a yell of pain.

'Who are you?' asked Tammy the next time they came round. He did not get his answer till they passed each other again.

'Sir Collywobble Crayfish, VIP,' called the stranger, and let out the painful yell once more.

'Mercy me! It's the Very Important Person,' cried Tammy as he whirled away. 'Poor soul! he sounds as if he has the collywobbles.'

'Always had the collywobbles,' said the VIP, whizzing past him. 'That's why I'm called Sir Collywobble. Get me out of this whirlpool, can't you? It's bad for my colly . . . wobbles. . . .'

Tammy's brains were going round and round, but they were still working, and suddenly he

thought of a bright idea. Perhaps if he bumped into Sir Collywobble it might knock them both off-course and pitch them out of the whirlpool.

Next time round he braced himself for a collision. 'Beg pardon, Sir Collywobble, I'm going to BUMP. . . .'

And bump he did, straight into the VIP's stomach. Sir Collywobble let out a loud yell as he and Tammy were tossed up into the air. But another miracle had happened, for when they came down they were safely out of the whirlpool and within sight of the Rubbish Heap.

'A miracle!' cried Sir Collywobble, patting his stomach. 'A marvellous miracle! You've cured my collywobbles. My tum feels ever so comfy. I haven't got a colly or a wobble left.' He gave a sigh of bliss. 'Ever so comfy! I'll have to change my name. What shall I call myself?'

'Sir Comfy Crayfish,' suggested Tammy, leading him towards the Rubbish Heap.

'I like it! What a splendid idea!' beamed Sir Comfy. 'You're a very bright fish. Indeed, you deserve the VC for being Very Clever.'

'Yes, I know,' said Tammy humbly. 'But I never boast about my brains, so let's drop the subject. Here we are, Sir Comfy. The reception committee's waiting for you.'

The tadpoles and tiddlers were all lined up in

rows of a thousand for inspection, and Granny was waiting with her feather boa round her neck and a diamond tiara on her head. Rab Rat and his whiskers were standing stiffly to attention and Froggy looked almost awake. PC Cod saluted so smartly that he knocked off his helmet, and a flock of starlings did a fly-past overhead.

'Yoo-hoo, Granny!' called the little fish. 'Get ready to curtsey, rheumatics permitting. Here comes Sir Comfy Crayfish, a VIP. And me a VC. We've been on a very circular tour. But now all's well that ends well. Thanks to me. Modesty prevents me from saying any more. Get on with the cheers!'

8
TAMMY TROOT'S SNOWMAN

I t was Katy Kipper who broke the news. She was on her way home from Hannah Herring's dancing-class when it suddenly started to snow. Katy had never seen snow before so it took her by surprise.

She rushed up to Tammy Troot and lisped, 'Oh! d'you thee what I thee? It'th raining white rain.'

'Don't be thilly, I mean silly!' scoffed Tammy. 'That's not rain. It's snow.'

'Thnow! Oh! it'th ever tho cold,' shivered Katy.

It grew colder and colder as the snow fell thicker and faster until the whole Rubbish Heap was covered with it. Granny had to fill her hot water bottle to keep her rheumatics warm. Rab Rat's whiskers were frozen into icicles, and there was no sign of Froggy until something stirred under a white blanket.

'Am I in the North — puff — Pole?' he wondered, opening a sleepy eye.

Soon the small fry were enjoying a snowball fight. Tammy Troot joined in till it became impossible to tell whether he was tossing tiddlers or snowballs. He blew on his cold fins and announced, 'I've got an idea!'

Rab groaned. 'Watch it, you lot,' he warned everybody. 'The Brain of Britain is about to speak.'

'What about building a Snowman?' suggested Tammy.

'Pass!' grunted Rab Rat.

Tammy took no notice of him. 'The exercise'll keep us warm, and there's plenty of junk in the Rubbish Heap to make a good base. Come on, everybody, all fins and paws to work!'

In spite of his grumbles Rab was soon as busy as the rest, fetching and carrying material to build the base of the Snowman. Old pots, pails, alarum-clocks, cocoa tins, jam jars and empty bottles. The snow soon covered the lot, and under Tammy's supervision a Snowman began to take shape.

'A very good shape,' said the little fish, standing on his tail to admire his masterpiece. 'I've seen worse in Parliament. Look! there's a pipe lying in the snow. Pop it in his mouth, Rab, and that'll add the finishing touch.'

The Snowman now looked so life-like that a Robin Redbreast, flying past the Rubbish Heap, cried, 'Oh! beg pardon, sir,' and changed course to avoid bumping into him.

The tadpoles and tiddlers took care not to hit him with their snowballs. Then suddenly Katy Kipper let out a scream. 'Oh! d'you thee what I thee? He'th thmoking hith pipe.'

'Nonsense!' Tammy Troot reproved her. 'Don't tell tarradiddles, Katy Kipper. How could a snowman . . . Jings! You're right.'

The Snowman *was* smoking. *Puff-puff-puff!* Great clouds of smoke were coming out of his pipe. *Puff-puff-puff!*

Tammy could not believe his eyes. Surely they must all be dreaming. Then he heard a clicking and a whirring as if all the bits and pieces inside the Snowman had begun to work. And now a very cocoa tinny voice spoke.

'Cold!' said the Snowman, beginning to shiver. 'Very cold!'

Tammy stared at him in amazement. 'Mercy me!' he gasped. 'I've made a mechanical snowman. Fancy that! Am I not a genius? Agreed! The answer's Yes!'

The Snowman was speaking again in his tinny voice. 'Cold!' he repeated. 'Very very cold!' He shook and shivered till all the pots and pans inside him began to rattle. 'Cold! Very VERY cold!'

Just then Tammy had one of his brainwaves. 'Hold on, Mr Snowman,' he cried. 'I'll go and fetch Granny's old mink shawl to keep you cosy. Don't move. I'll be right back.'

The Snowman stood still and smoked his pipe — *puff-puff-puff* — while Tammy hurried away and came rushing back with a warm woolly shawl lined with mink.

'Here you are, Mr Snowman,' he said. 'With Granny's compliments.'

The Snowman said, 'Thank you, Granny,' in a cracked voice. Then when the shawl was round his shoulders he gave a satisfied sigh and seemed to fall asleep. Not another word did he say. No more *puff-puff-puffs* from his pipe. No sound of whirring from inside. Not even the smallest snore.

Tammy was beginning to wonder if he had imagined it all. Were they all sound asleep like the Snowman? Perhaps *he* was frozen, too, into a snow-fish. Then he heard someone breathing behind him. It was Katy Kipper in a great state of alarm.

'Oh! d'you thee what I thee?' she said in a frightened whisper. 'We've got a vithitor. I think it'th a — a Polar Bear.'

'Don't tell tarradiddles, Katy Kipper,' Tammy began to scold her. Then he stopped himself and gaped at the visitor. It *was* a Polar Bear.

A large white Polar Bear who came padding into the Rubbish Heap on his great paws. Then he reared himself up on his hind legs and spoke in a growly voice.

'Fee-fi-fo-fum! Heat for my body and food for my tum.' He gave an angry roar. 'D'you hear me? Fetch them at once. Heat for my body, food for my tum. Fee-fi-fo-fum. Spring to it!'

There was no one to spring to it except Tammy Troot. Everyone else had sunk below the surface in terror, hidden behind the Snowman or escaped to the safety of the cave. So the little fish was left to face the Polar Bear on his own. But he was used to danger. 'Play for time, Tammy Troot,' he told himself, trying his best to keep calm.

'I'm springing to it, Mr Polar Bear, sir,' he said, saluting with his fin. 'I tell you what, I could bring you Granny's hot water bottle, if you like. I'm sure she wouldn't mind lending it to you in a g-good c-cause. How does that ap-peal to you?'

'Bring your Granny, too,' growled the Polar Bear, licking his lips. 'She'll fill up a corner for a start and take the edge off my appetite. Then you can fill up another. Spring to it! I'm getting hungrier and colder. Colder and hungrier. Fee-fi-fo-fum. Heat for my body and food for my tum!'

Tammy saluted again, wondering what his next move should be. Poor Granny! He had no intention of sacrificing her; but how could *he* escape? Was this to be the sad end of the Brain of Britain? No! someone would come to his aid. Who would it be?

The Snowman! The Polar Bear was taking a quick look at him, standing still as a statue with the cosy shawl round his shoulders.

'Spring to it!' he growled. 'Give me that shawl. It'll keep out the cold wind till I get the hot water bottle. D'you hear me? Spring to it!'

The Snowman took no notice, so the Polar Bear put out an impatient paw and snatched the shawl from his back. Then he jumped back with a howl of horror, for in touching the Snowman he had set

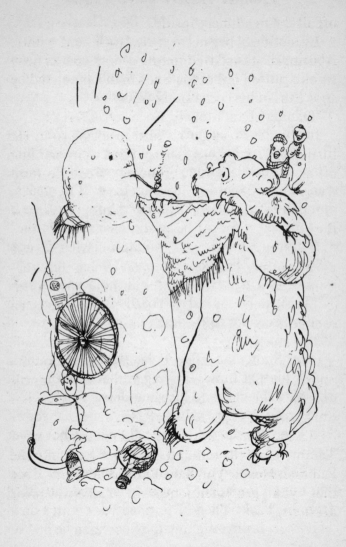

off all the machinery inside.

Everything began to tick, tock and whirr. Alarum-clocks started to ting-a-ling, sparks flew, smoke puffed out of the Snowman's pipe, and he spoke up in his cocoa tinny voice.

'Danger! Don't touch! Go away! AWAY!'

It was the Polar Bear's turn to spring to it. He turned tail, dropped the shawl and went padding off as fast as he could, growling, 'Fee-fi-fo-fum! Away I go with an empty tum. Good . . . bye. . . .'

'Hooray!' cheered Tammy Troot. 'Saved by the bell!'

He went to pick up Granny's shawl and was about to thank the Snowman for saving the situation when Katy Kipper came rushing up to him.

'Oh! d'you thee what I thee?' she said in an excited voice. 'The thun'th coming out.'

The sun!

Out it came, beaming so brightly that soon the Snowman began to melt. The pipe fell from his mouth, and all Tammy could hear was a faint tinny voice saying 'Ta . . . ta. . . .'

'Ta-ta, Mr Snowman, and thanks,' cried Tammy as all the bits and pieces fell back into the Rubbish Heap. 'You haven't lived in vain. I'll see that you get mentioned in *Tammy Troot's Memoirs*.'

9
TAMMY TROOT'S TEAPOT

Granny Troot was getting ready to go to a Second-Hand Sale when Tammy came scurrying up the burn.

'Take cover, everybody!' he cried. 'Here comes Mrs Flounder and her spoilt brat, Willy-Nilly.'

'Mrs Flounder's coming to the Second-Hand Sale with me,' said Granny, putting on her shawl. 'So you'll have to look after Willy-Nilly while she's away. And don't get up to any tricks, Tammy Troot, for you know how fond she is of Willy-Nilly. She hardly ever lets him out of her sight.'

'Oh jings!' groaned Tammy. 'That's my day ruined.' But he had no time to protest before Mrs Flounder arrived, holding Willy-Nilly by the fin.

'Hullo, Tammy-Pammy,' she gushed. 'You'll take good care of my little fishy-wishy, won't you? Mammy's wee pet! Ta-ta, Willy-Nilly. Give your Mammy-Pammy a little kissy-wissy.'

Willy-Nilly burst into floods of tears. 'Boo-hoo! Don't want to leave my Mammy-Pammy. Boo-hoo!'

Tammy Troot sighed. He would have liked to

suggest giving Willy-Nilly a good spanking. Instead, to save the situation, he suggested playing a game, and used a bit of flattery at the same time.

'Hide and seek! Come on, Willy-Nilly. I bet you're a champion, eh? I won't stand a chance against you, will I?'

'No, no! Not a chance!' The flattery worked. Willy-Nilly dried his eyes and said, 'I'm a very clever little fishy-wishy. My Mammy-Pammy says so. You'll never catch me. No, you'll never! Close your eyes, Tammy-Pammy.'

As Granny and Mrs Flounder went off to the Sale, Tammy obligingly closed his eyes. 'Give me strength!' he sighed to himself. 'I wish he'd get lost, and the loster the better. He's a perfect pesty-westy.'

But when he opened his eyes and saw no sign of Willy-Nilly, he began to feel alarmed. What would Mrs Flounder say if her precious pet really *did* get lost? He started to hunt high and low, but without any luck.

'Wi-lly-Ni-lly' he called out in a worried voice. 'Where are you? Speak to me.'

No reply.

Then suddenly Tammy caught sight of an old china teapot whose lid was rattling violently. A faint cry was coming from inside.

'Help! The lid's got stuck. Boo-hoo! Let me out! I want my Mammy-Pammy! Boo-hoo!'

Tammy was rushing to the rescue when the telephone gave a loud *ting-a-ling*. 'Hold on, Willy-Nilly. I'll be with you in two toots,' he cried, and picked up the receiver. 'Rubbish Heap 1212. State your business.'

It was Mrs Flounder herself who stated her business. 'Is that you, Tammy-Pammy? Could I have a word with Willy-Nilly? I just want to be sure my wee pet's all right. Is he missing his Mammy-Pammy, the little darling? You're taking good care of him, I hope?'

Tammy said hastily, 'Oh yes, Mrs Flounder.

Ever such good care. In fact, he's enjoying himself so much he hasn't got t-time to c-come to the t-t-telephone.'

No wonder Tammy started to stutter. From the corner of his eye he had just seen the teapot start to sail away down the burn. Willy-Nilly was rattling feverishly at the lid and screaming for help. The best thing Tammy could do was shout into the telephone to cover up the sound.

'Are you still there, Mrs Flounder? This is an awful bad line. I think I'd better ring off. Ch-Cheerio, and don't worry about wee Willy-Nilly. He's having the t-time of his l-life. Good-bye!'

Tammy banged down the receiver before Mrs Flounder could say another word. Then away he dashed after the teapot. But it was gathering so much speed that no matter how fast he went he could not catch up with it. Then, to his horror, he saw it was making straight for the cave where the Second-Hand Sale was being held. Before he could stop it the teapot had lodged itself beside a heap of junk waiting to be sold.

'Oh help!' thought Tammy. 'Never a dull moment!'

He could see his Granny and Mrs Flounder amongst the crowd, listening to every word the auctioneer was saying.

'What am I bid for this old-fashioned soup

ladle?' he was asking. 'In excellent condition. Genuine antique. Solid silver.'

'Fiddlesticks!' Tammy could hear his Granny contradicting. 'No such thing. It's genuine tin, and cracked at that.'

Mrs Flounder was not interested in the soup ladle. She had caught sight of the teapot and taken a sudden fancy to it. So had a stout foreign dealer, called Mr Antonio, who wanted to buy it for his collection.

'Mister sir!' he shouted out to the auctioneer. 'You no bother about the soup ladle. You sell me, Antonio, the kettle-pot. Antonio, he give you good price. Feefty pence! Going, going, gone! Sold to Mr Antonio. One kettle-pot for feefty pence!'

And before Mrs Flounder could start bidding against him the deed was done. The teapot now belonged to Mr Antonio, who took possession of it at once and began trundling it down the burn in the direction of goodness-knows-where.

What was Tammy to do? 'Oh mercy me! I'll have to stop him before Willy-Nilly gets hi-jacked.' And he went hurrying away after the foreigner, calling out, 'Mr Antonio! Mr Antonio, sir! Could you hold on a moment, please?'

Mr Antonio turned round and said, 'Yes, yes! I hold on. What you want, young Mr Troot? You

sell me cheap bargain? For feefty pence?'

'No, no, Mr Antonio,' said Tammy. 'I was only wanting to congratulate you on your bravery.'

Mr Antonio looked surprised. 'Antonio, he is brave, yes?'

'Very brave,' Tammy told him craftily. 'After all, it's not everyone who would dare to buy a haunted teapot.'

Mr Antonio gave him a startled look. 'What you say? The kettle-pot he is haunted? You mean there is a g-g-ghost inside?'

Tammy answered truthfully. 'Well, there's somebody inside, Mr Antonio. You can hear for yourself. Listen!'

At that moment the teapot lid began to rattle and a faint, tearful voice was heard wailing, 'Mammy! Let me out! I want my Mammy-Pammy! Boo-hoo!'

That was enough for Mr Antonio. 'Is bad bargain,' he cried, leaping back from the teapot. 'Antonio, he lose his feefty pence, but he no care. Antonio, he no like ghosts. You keep the kettle-pot. Antonio, he is going, going, gone . . . .'

And he was gone in the twinkling of a second, leaving Tammy in possession of the haunted teapot. He was pushing it back up the burn when he almost bumped into Mrs Flounder, who had just left the Second-Hand Sale.

… …lounder,' he said innocently.
… …esent for you.'

… …sent!' Mrs Flounder clapped her fins
… …ght. 'Oh my! Are you not a clever little
…ishy! That's the very thing I wanted to buy.
How did you guess, Tammy-Pammy? I thought that foreign dealer had bought it, but I'm delighted to see it. DELIGHTED! And, by the way, how's Willy-Nilly, the little darling? You haven't been neglecting Mammy's wee pet?'

Tammy handed over the teapot to her and said, 'No, no, far from it, Mrs Flounder. Mammy's wee pet's safe and sound. If you look inside the teapot you'll get a pleasant surprise. A surprise, anyway! I won't say it hasn't been a pleasure looking after Willy-Nilly. I'll just say ta-ta and go away home to give my brains a resty-pesty.'

10
TAMMY TROOT'S TELEGRAM

One day the Pigeon Postie came flying over the burn. He had an important look on his face and a telegram tucked under his wing.

'Special delivery for Tammy Troot Esquire! Are you there, Tammy? Catch!' He dropped the telegram and flew off to deliver the rest of his mail.

Tammy looked up as something came tumbling down from the sky, and caught it neatly in his fin. But it was not the telegram. It was one of the Pigeon Postie's tail feathers.

Where was the telegram? There it was, fluttering away downstream, swirling round corners and gathering speed. 'Mercy! I'd better scoot after it,' cried Tammy. 'It might be something very important. Maybe I've come into a fortune or been made Prime Minister. I'll have to find out.'

He gathered speed, too. So much speed that he almost knocked Granny flat on her face as she was coming back from the supermarket with a laden basket.

'Watch where you're going, Tammy Troot,' she cried angrily. 'You've bumped into my rheumatics. Have you nothing better to do than chase a piece of paper down the burn?'

'It's a telegram,' said Tammy hastily. 'I'll have to keep it in sight.' He presented her with the Postie's tail feather. 'Put that in your hat, Granny. Ta-ta; I'm away at the toot.'

It was not easy to keep the telegram in sight, for by now a breeze had blown it up on to a hedge. Then away it flew over the hedge into a turnip field. It was lucky that a little stream trickled through the field. Tammy followed at full speed just in time to see the telegram fly up and land in the breast pocket of a scarecrow standing guard over the turnips.

'Er – excuse me, Mr Scarecrow, sir,' said Tammy, looking up at him. 'I wonder if you could oblige me by giving me back my telegram?'

'I'll do better than that,' said the scarecrow in a very rusty voice. It was a long time since he had spoken to anyone. 'I'll read it to you. Hold on a jiffy till I find my specs. Now where did I put them? It's years since I had them on.'

He was fumbling through all his pockets when a large black crow came swooping down from the sky.

'Caw! Caw! I'll have that!' he croaked, catching sight of the telegram. 'It'll make a nice lining for my nest. Caw! Caw!' And he snatched the telegram and flew off with it in his beak.

Tammy's heart sank as he watched the crow fly away into the distance. But he was not one to give in. 'Never say die, Tammy Troot,' he told himself. 'I'll go and yoke my helicopter. Cheerio, Mr Scarecrow. I'll wave to you as I fly past.'

He rushed back to the Rubbish Heap where the old kettle he used as a helicopter was parked. Soon he was in the air with sparks flying and smoke coming out of the spout, making straight for the treetops. He waved to the scarecrow as he

flew past, then he flew around, peering into all the nests until at last he saw the crow sitting sound asleep on the telegram.

'Wakey-wakey!' called Tammy, hovering near the nest. But the crow only tucked his beak under his wing and gave a sleepy SN-O-O-O-RE.

Tammy puzzled his brains. What was he to do? Perhaps a direct hit might dislodge the telegram.

It did! Tammy backed his kettle and revved up. Then he aimed straight for the nest. CRASH! The impact dislodged not only the telegram but also the crow, who gave a loud 'CAW!' as he was rudely awakened from his sleep.

'Beg pardon, Mr Crow,' cried Tammy, flying away after the telegram. 'Sorry to disturb your dreams, but this is an emergency. Stop, telegram, stop!'

The telegram had no intention of stopping. It seemed to be in a more frisky mood after having a rest in the crow's nest. It flew away above the chimney tops, it turned cartwheels in the air, it rose and fell till Tammy was almost air-sick, trying to follow it.

'Bless my brains! It's like an obstacle race,' groaned the little fish. 'I never knew a telegram could cut such capers.'

But all of a sudden it seemed to run out of steam and down-down-down it fell, floating over a high

wall and landing in a pool of water. Tammy quickly followed it, touched down in the pool, and was reaching over to grab the telegram when he heard a strange noise.

Not just one noise. A mixture of frightening noises, like the roaring of wild beasts.

'Mercy me! Is this the jungle?' he gasped. 'That sounds like a t-tiger. And is that an el-elephant? Oh! that's a l-lion! Goodness gracious! I've landed in the zoo.'

True enough! When he looked around him he could see a camel swaying about, a zebra kicking up his heels, and a squad of penguins parading straight to the pool where he had landed.

'Oh jings! I'm in the danger zone,' he told himself, ducking down inside his kettle. 'Keep your head, Tammy Troot. The future looks awful unsettled.'

So did the present! The penguins were coming nearer, marching in single file, like little gentlemen in evening dress, with a big bossy bird at their head. He was rapping out orders in a commanding voice.

'Left-right! Left-right! Keep in step, you lot! Right-left! Right-left! Wait for it! Now! Jump in!'

There was a great splash as the penguins entered the pool. Tammy's kettle began to bob about on the surface and the telegram floated away out of his reach.

'Oh, see that!' cried the leader, setting off after it.

'Oh, see that!' echoed the rest of the penguins. 'Something to eat!'

'It's mine!' screamed the bossy penguin, picking it up in his beak. 'I saw it first.'

'No! it's mine! It's mine!' The other penguins gathered round him and tried to tear it from his beak. They all screamed and squabbled as they fought for possession of the telegram. And before long it was pecked into a hundred pieces, like a jigsaw puzzle that could never be put together again.

'That's torn it!' sighed Tammy, watching the pieces floating away. 'Oh dear! Now I'll never know what the message was. But the main thing is to get away at the toot before *I* get pecked to pieces.'

Too late! The bossy penguin, having swallowed part of the telegram, was now looking round for something else to eat.

'Oh! see that!' he cried, splashing towards Tammy's helicopter. 'It's mine! I spotted it first.'

'No! it's mine! It's mine!' screamed the others, hurrying after him. And once more they began to squabble.

'Save your breath!' called Tammy. 'You're all

wrong. It's mine!'

And as the penguins came peck-peck-pecking at the kettle, he revved up his engine and blew out a great cloud of smoke through the spout.

'Can't see! Can't see!' screamed the penguins, and they began peck-peck-pecking at each other while the helicopter suddenly took off. Tammy whizzed past an elephant, narrowly missed a camel and flew safely away from the zoo.

'Hooray! Another near miss!' cried Tammy Troot as he went zooming away back home. 'Mind! Though I say it myself, I'm a champion at getting out of tight corners.'

He had reached the crossroads in the burn when he looked down and saw a familiar figure struggling along with a heavy bundle on his back.

'It's my Uncle Geordie from Glasgow! What on earth is he doing here? I wonder if he's coming to visit us? I hope so, for he always brings such nice presents.' Tammy swooped down and called, 'Hullo, Uncle Geordie! D'you want a lift? Hop in!'

Uncle Geordie mopped his brow and gave a sigh of relief as he got into the helicopter with his bundle.

'Good for you, Tammas!' he beamed. 'Right on time! This parcel of presents was awful heavy. Isn't it a blessing I sent that telegram asking you to meet me here?'

'Oh yes, Uncle Geordie,' agreed Tammy, smiling to himself. 'They're wonderful things, telegrams!'